The Lady in the Lake

RAYMOND CHANDLER

Level 2

Retold by Jennifer Bassett
Series Editors: Andy Hopkins and Jocelyn Potter

Pearson Education Limited
Edinburgh Gate, Harlow,
Essex CM20 2JE, England
and Associated Companies throughout the world.

ISBN: 978-1-4058-6975-1

Typeset by Graphicraft Ltd, Hong Kong
Set in 11/14pt Bembo
Printed and bound in Great Britain by Ashford Colour Press Ltd
SWTC/01

Published by Pearson Education Ltd in association with
Penguin Books Ltd, both companies being subsidiaries of Pearson Plc

Contents

Introduction

She's dangerous, that lady. She eats men for breakfast, but they love it. One smile from her and men jump out of windows for her.

Derace Kingsley's wife, Crystal, left Los Angeles and went to their second house in the mountains for a week or two. But she didn't come back. Now Philip Marlowe, a Los Angeles detective, is looking for her. Did she go to El Paso with her lover or is she dead? Did her lover kill her? Is she the lady in the lake? Or is that another woman, Muriel Chess? Marlowe has to find answers – and quickly. Because there is a murderer in Los Angeles, and Marlowe is finding too many dead bodies.

Raymond Chandler is one of America's most famous detective writers. He was born in Chicago, Illinois, in 1888. When he was nine, his mother took him to England. He went to school there and later worked for British newspapers. He went back to America in 1912. From 1917 he fought in Europe in the First World War (1914–18) with the Canadians.

In 1919, he went back to the US and lived in California. He got married and had an important job in a big company. At the age of forty-four, he lost his job and started to write detective stories for magazines. He sold his first story in 1933. His first book, *The Big Sleep* (1939), was about a detective, Philip Marlowe. People liked the book very much, and Chandler wrote many more books about Marlowe. *Farewell My Lovely* (1940), *The High Window* (1942), *The Lady in the Lake* (1944) and *The Long Goodbye* (1953) are some of America's best detective stories. There are films of many of his stories. After his wife died in 1954, Chandler was very unhappy. He drank a lot and was very ill. He died in 1959.

Chapter 1   Where Is Crystal?

The man in front of me was tall and strong, with thick dark hair. He sat in an expensive chair behind an expensive desk, and looked at me with cold grey eyes. He didn't have time to smile.

'OK, Marlowe,' he said. 'So you're a private detective. One of the best in Los Angeles, I hear. I have a job for you. I want you to find my wife. Think you can do that?'

I sat back in my chair and lit a cigarette slowly.

'Yes, Mr Kingsley,' I said. 'I think I can do that.'

'How much?'

'Twenty-five dollars a day. Half a dollar a mile for my car. And a hundred in my hand now, before I do anything.'

He looked at me, and I looked back at him and waited.

Then he smiled. 'OK, Marlowe, you've got the job. But don't talk about it to the police. I have an important job here.' He looked round his quiet, expensive office. The hot July sun didn't get into this room. 'I want to stay in this job, and I can't have any trouble with the police.'

'Is your wife in trouble?' I asked.

'I don't know. Perhaps. She sometimes does very stupid things, and she has dangerous friends.'

He gave me a drink and told me the story. 'I have a house in the mountains, near Puma Point. Crystal went up there in May. She often meets her men friends up there.' He looked at me. 'She has a lot of men friends . . . you understand? But there was an important dinner down here on June 12th, and Crystal didn't come back for it.'

'So what did you do?'

'Nothing. Because of this.' He gave me a letter and I read it.

El Paso, 14th June

I'm leaving you and going to Mexico. I'm going to marry Chris Lavery. Good luck and goodbye. Crystal.

'I wasn't very unhappy about that,' Kingsley said. 'She can have him, and he can have her. Then two weeks later I heard from the Prescott Hotel in San Bernardino. Crystal's car was there and they wanted money for it. But yesterday I met Lavery, here in town. He didn't know anything about Crystal, and he last saw her two months ago. So where *is* she? What happened to her?'

I thought about it for a minute or two, and then I asked him some questions. We talked for about half an hour. Kingsley gave me a photo of his wife with Chris Lavery – it was a good picture of Lavery, but not very good of the lady.

I finished my drink and stood up. 'OK, Mr Kingsley, I'm going to talk to Lavery, and then go up to your house in the mountains.'

'My house is at Little Fawn Lake,' he told me. 'A man works for me up there – Bill Chess is his name. And the girl at the telephone desk outside can help you. She knows a lot of my wife's friends. Talk to her. And you can phone me any time – day or night.'

Outside Kingsley's office I looked at the girl at the telephone desk. She was small and pretty, with short red hair and blue eyes. I like redheads. I gave her my best smile.

'Hi, blue eyes,' I said. 'Your boss says you know a lot of people. Tell me about Chris Lavery.'

'Chris Lavery? What do you want to know?'

'Anything. Do you like him?'

'Well,' she said, 'he has a beautiful body.'

'And all the girls like a man with a beautiful body, eh?'

She laughed. 'Perhaps. But I know nicer men than Chris Lavery. He knows too many women.'

We talked for about ten minutes. Kingsley was right. Redhead knew a lot of people and she liked talking. Perhaps her job wasn't

I started with Lavery. He didn't want to talk to me, but nobody wants to talk to private detectives.

very interesting. I sat on her desk and listened, and smiled into her blue eyes. She smiled back.

Then I stood up. 'Well, I must go. See you again, blue eyes.'

Redhead laughed happily. 'Any time, Mr Marlowe.'

♦

I started with Lavery. He was at home, at 623 Altair Street, down in Bay City. He didn't want to talk to me, but nobody wants to talk to private detectives.

'No,' he told me angrily. 'I didn't go to El Paso with Crystal Kingsley. OK, so we sleep together. But I don't want to marry her. She's very rich, and money is nice, but Crystal's a difficult lady. I last saw her about two months ago.'

I sat and watched him. 'So why did she write that letter from El Paso?'

'Don't know. She likes playing games – stupid games.'

It wasn't a very good story, and he knew it. I asked him some more questions, but his story stayed the same. I went out and sat in my car outside his house. I thought about Lavery. Perhaps he went away with Mrs Kingsley, and then they had a fight. But where did Mrs Kingsley go after that?

A big black Cadillac drove up and stopped at the house across the street. A thin man with a black doctor's bag got out and went into the house. I looked at the name on the door – Dr Albert S. Almore. Doctors know a lot about people. Perhaps this one knew Lavery. I saw Dr Almore at the window. He watched me carefully, and his face was angry and afraid. Then he sat down and made a telephone call, but he watched me all the time.

Five minutes later a green car came along and stopped at the doctor's house. The driver walked across the road to my car.

'Waiting for somebody?' he asked.

'I don't know,' I said. 'Am I?'

'Don't get clever with me,' he said coldly. 'I'm Detective Degarmo, Bay City Police. Why are you watching Dr Almore's house?

I looked out of my car window at him. He was a big man with a square face and very blue eyes.

'What's all this about?' I asked. 'I don't know Dr Almore, and I'm not interested in him. I'm visiting a friend. What's the doctor afraid of?'

'I ask the questions, not you,' he said. 'Go on – get out of here. Move!' He walked away and went into Dr Almore's house.

Back in Los Angeles, I phoned Mr Kingsley and asked him about Dr Albert S. Almore.

'I'm Detective Degarmo, Bay City Police,' he said. He was a big man with a square face and very blue eyes.

'I don't know him, but he was Crystal's doctor for a time,' he told me. 'His wife died a year and a half ago – she killed herself. It was very sad.'

I got into my car again and started for the mountains. Dr Almore was afraid of something, but what?

Chapter 2   The Lady in the Lake

I drove through the hot afternoon to San Bernardino, then up into the mountains. Past the village of Puma Point I took the road up to Little Fawn Lake. The road was slow and difficult through the mountains, and soon there were no more houses or people.

When I got to the lake, I stopped at the nearest house and got out. A man came out and walked across to me. He was a heavy man, not very tall, and he had a hard, city face.

'Bill Chess?' I asked.

'That's me.'

'I want to look at Mr Kingsley's house,' I said. 'I have a letter for you from him.'

He read the letter carefully, and then I asked him some questions about the house. He was happy to talk to me.

'I don't see many people up here,' he said. He looked at the blue sky and the mountains, and his eyes were sad. 'No friends. No wife. Nothing.'

I got a bottle of whisky from my car, and we sat together in the evening sun and drank. I'm a good listener.

'No wife,' Bill Chess said again. He looked into his glass of whisky. 'She left me. She left me a month ago. The 12th of June.'

I gave him some more whisky and sat quietly. June 12th – the

I got a bottle of whisky from my car, and we sat together in the evening sun and drank. I'm a good listener.

day when Mrs Kingsley didn't go back to Los Angeles for the dinner.

'Tell me about it,' I said quietly.

He drank his whisky quickly. It was not his first drink that day. 'I met Muriel a year and three months ago,' he said slowly. 'We married three weeks later. I loved her a lot, but . . . well, I was stupid. Here I am – I've got a good job, a pretty little wife, so what do I do?' He looked across the lake at the Kingsleys' house. 'I get into bed with that Kingsley cat over there. OK, she's as pretty as Muriel – the same long yellow hair, same eyes, same nice little body – but she's nothing to me. But Muriel knows all about it. So we had a fight, and that night she left me. I went out, and when I got home, there was a letter on the table. "Goodbye, Bill," she says, "I don't want to live with you after this." '

He finished his whisky. 'I didn't see the Kingsley woman again. She went down the mountain that same night. And not a word from Muriel now for a month.' He turned and looked at me. 'It's an old story,' he said, 'but thanks for listening.'

I put the whisky bottle back in the car, and together we walked round the lake to the Kingsleys' house. I looked round the house, but there was nothing interesting for me there.

'Perhaps Mrs Kingsley went away with your wife,' I said to Bill Chess.

He thought about it for a minute. 'No,' he said. 'Muriel never liked that Kingsley cat.'

We walked on round the lake. There were only two other houses and there was nobody in them. It was quiet and clean and beautiful by that lake, away from the hot, dirty city. We stopped by an old boat and looked down into the water at the fish.

Suddenly Bill Chess caught my arm. 'Look!' he said. 'Look down there!' His hand was heavy on my arm, and his face was white.

I looked, and about ten feet below the water I saw something yellow. Something long and yellow. It moved slowly through the water. A woman's hair.

I started to say something, but Bill Chess jumped into the lake and swam down under the water. He pulled and pushed, and quickly came up again through the water. The body followed him slowly. A body in red trousers and a black jacket. A body with a grey-white face, without eyes, without mouth, just long yellow hair. It was not a pretty thing – after a month in the water.

'Muriel!' said Bill Chess. Suddenly he was an old, old man. He sat there by the lake with his head in his hands. 'It's Muriel!' he said, again and again.

♦

Down in Puma Point village, the police station was just a one-room little house. The name on the door said, 'JIM PATTON – POLICE'. I went in.

Jim Patton was a big slow man, with a big round face and a big slow smile. He spoke slowly and he thought slowly, but his eyes weren't stupid. I liked everything about him.

I lit a cigarette and told him about the dead woman in Little Fawn Lake.

'Bill Chess's wife – Muriel,' I said. 'She and Bill had a fight a month ago, then she left him. She wrote him a letter – a goodbye letter, or a suicide letter. I don't know.'

Jim Patton looked at me. 'OK,' he said slowly. 'Let's go and talk to Bill. And who are you, son?'

'Marlowe. I'm a private detective from LA. I'm working for Mr Kingsley. He wants me to find his wife.'

We drove up to the lake with the doctor and the police boys in the back of the car.

*Bill Chess was a very unhappy man. 'You think I murdered Muriel?'
he said angrily to Patton.*

Bill Chess was a very unhappy man. 'You think that *I* murdered Muriel?' he said angrily to Patton.

'Perhaps you did, and perhaps you didn't,' said Patton sadly. 'But I must take you down to the police station, Bill. There's going to be a lot of questions.'

Chapter 3   Al to Mildred

I had dinner at the hotel in Puma Point. When I finished, a girl came up to my table. I didn't know her.

She smiled at me. 'Can I sit with you for a minute, Mr Marlowe?' she asked.

I got out my cigarettes. 'Word gets round fast in small villages,' I said. 'What do you want to talk about?'

She smiled again. 'About Bill Chess. Do you think he murdered Muriel?'

'I don't know. Perhaps. But I'm not interested in Bill or Muriel Chess.'

'No?' The girl put out her cigarette. 'Listen to this, then. There was a Los Angeles policeman – De Soto – up here about six weeks ago. Big man with a square face. Said he wanted to find a woman with the name Mildred Haviland. He had a photograph with him. We thought the photo was Muriel Chess. OK, the hair was red-brown, but a woman can easily change the colour of her hair. Nobody here liked this De Soto, so we didn't tell him anything. What do you think about that?'

I lit another cigarette. 'But I don't know a Mildred Haviland. And I never heard of Muriel Chess before today.'

'Bill Chess isn't a bad man,' she said quietly. 'We like him, and we don't think he's a murderer.'

When she left, I found a telephone and called Derace Kingsley. His answers to my questions didn't help. No, he

11

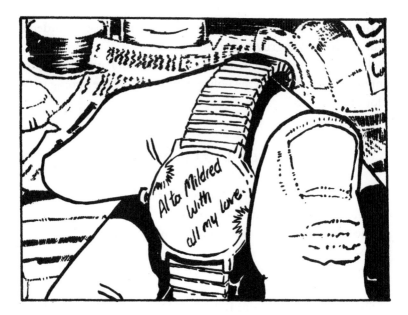

*And in the tin of sugar I found a watch with some words on the
back of it: 'Al to Mildred. With all my love.'*

didn't know Muriel Chess very well. Yes, his wife was friendly
with Muriel. No, he didn't know a woman called Mildred
Haviland.

It was dark when I got back to Bill Chess's house by Little Fawn
Lake. I went in quietly through a back window, and looked round
the house very carefully. Why was I interested in Bill Chess's wife? I
didn't know, but she knew Mrs Kingsley, she lived in the same place,
and she 'went away' on the same day. Perhaps that was important,
and perhaps it wasn't.

In the kitchen I looked in all the cupboards and through the tins
of food. And in the tin of sugar I found a small, very pretty watch
inside some paper. On the back of the watch there were some
words: *Al to Mildred. With all my love.*

Al to Mildred. Al somebody to Mildred Haviland. Mildred Haviland was Muriel Chess. Muriel Chess was dead – two weeks after a policeman called De Soto came to Puma Point with her photograph. I stood there and thought about it. Mrs Kingsley didn't come in to this story.

I drove back down to Puma Point and went in to Jim Patton's office. I put the little watch on his desk.

'I looked round Bill Chess's house,' I said, 'and I found this in a tin of sugar.'

Jim Patton looked at me sadly. 'Are you going to give me trouble, son? I looked round the house and didn't find anything. But your eyes are younger than mine.' He looked carefully at the little watch. 'So what do *you* think about this?' he asked me.

'I don't think Bill Chess murdered his wife. I don't think he knew she had another name. But somebody from her past looked for her and found her. With a new name and a new husband. He didn't like that, and so he murdered her.'

Jim Patton thought about it. 'Mmm,' he said slowly. 'I like it. The story begins well, but how does it finish?'

'Ask me tomorrow,' I said.

Jim Patton laughed. 'You city detectives are too fast for us slow mountain people. Goodnight, son.'

♦

At about eleven that night I drove into San Bernardino and found the Prescott Hotel. The garage boy was happy to talk to me – when he had some of my dollars in his dirty hand. He looked at the photo of Crystal Kingsley and Chris Lavery.

'Yeah, I remember the man,' he said. 'He came up to the woman at the hotel desk. But this photo's not very good of the woman. A woman with the name Mrs Kingsley left her car here on the evening of June the 12th, and took a taxi to the station that night, with the man. She wore a black-and-white dress, with a

13

black-and-white hat, and she was small and pretty with long yellow hair. Perhaps she was the woman in this photo, but I don't know.'

I thanked him and gave him two more dollars for luck.

It was too hot in San Bernardino, so I got back in my car and drove home to Hollywood. I got in at a quarter to three in the morning. I had a bath, went to bed and slept well.

Chapter 4   A Pretty Lady's Gun

In the morning I drank a lot of black coffee and made some phone calls. A good friend of mine worked in the city police offices. There was no detective with the name of De Soto in the city of Los Angeles, he told me. I phoned Kingsley's office, said hello to Redhead, and then told Kingsley about Lavery and the Prescott Hotel.

'What are you going to do now?' he asked me.

'Go and talk to Lavery again,' I said. 'He met your wife in San Bernardino on June 12th, so I want a better story from him today.'

I drove down to Bay City and stopped the car up the street from Lavery's house. I smoked a cigarette and though about Lavery. Then I saw a woman at Lavery's front door. She came out, closed the door quietly behind her and walked away down the street. She wore dark glasses, a brown coat and a light-blue hat. I didn't see her face, but her hair was dark brown and she had very nice legs. I like legs. I watched them all down the street.

Lavery's front door was shut, but I gave it a little push with my finger, and it opened. I went in and called his name, but there was no answer. I walked round the house and had a look in his bedroom. There was a very big bed in there, but Lavery wasn't in it. I looked into some of the cupboards – shoes, jackets, shirts, trousers . . . and a

14

Then I saw a woman at Lavery's front door. She came out, closed the door quietly behind her and walked away down the street.

woman's dress. An expensive black-and-white dress, with a nice little black-and-white hat. I closed the cupboard quietly, and opened another door at the back of the room. Inside was a bathroom, and Lavery *was* at home.

He was in the bath, and he was very, very dead. There was a gun on the floor – a small, pretty lady's gun, but it can kill as well as any other gun. I looked round the bathroom. There wasn't a fight – Lavery knew his killer. She opened the door, came in and shot him three or four times. Not Lavery's lucky day.

I took the little gun with me and went out to my car. The street was quiet and sunny, no police cars, no policemen. Only Marlowe, finding another dead body. Murder-a-day Marlowe, they call him. I got into my car and drove away from there fast.

♦

In his quiet, expensive office Derace Kingsley listened to me with a white face.

'Did your wife have a gun?' I asked.

'Yes.'

'Is this it?' I showed him the gun from the floor in Lavery's bathroom.

He looked at it, and then at me. 'I don't know. Perhaps. But Crystal isn't a murderer – she didn't kill Lavery!'

'Why not? The police are going to think she did. She was with Lavery in San Bernardino. They didn't go to Mexico. Then perhaps one day she sees him with another woman. So she gets angry, and goes round to his house. She leaves the gun on the floor, her dress in the cupboard . . . The police are going to love it.' I stood up and looked down at him. 'I must take the gun back now and call the police. I can't cover up a murder.'

Kingsley said nothing and put his head in his hands. Then he looked up at me. 'Listen, Marlowe,' he said quietly. 'You're working for me, right? I *know* Crystal didn't kill Lavery! What about that

Lavery was in the bath, and he was very, very dead. There was a gun on the floor – a small pretty lady's gun.

woman in the blue hat? Who was she? Lavery knew a lot of women. Go and find the murderer. Show the police that Crystal didn't kill Lavery. Do that, and there's five hundred dollars for you.'

'OK, Mr Kingsley,' I said. 'But the job gets more difficult every day.'

When I went out, the redhead at the telephone desk called to me. 'Mr Marlowe,' she said quickly, 'yesterday you wanted to know about Dr Almore. Mr Kingsley told me. Well, I talked to some friends last night.'

I went over and sat on her desk. 'OK, blue eyes, tell me.'

'Some rich women drink a lot, and take drugs. They think it's exciting,' she began. 'Sometimes they take too much and get ill. Well, people say that Dr Almore helps these women. He gives them different drugs, they get better . . . and Dr Almore gets a lot of money. Florence Almore, his wife, took drugs, too. She wasn't a very nice woman. One night, a year and a half ago, she came home ill. Dr Almore's office nurse put her to bed, but later that night Mrs Almore walked down to the garage. Chris Lavery found the body. When he came home, he heard the sound of a car in the Almores' garage. He opened the door and found her dead on the floor. Dr Almore was out. The police say it was suicide. But some people say it was murder. Florence Almore's parents thought it was murder.'

She looked up at me with her big blue eyes. 'Does that help you, Mr Marlowe?'

'Yes,' I said slowly, 'I think it does.' I gave her a big smile. 'You and I must have dinner together some time, blue eyes.'

♦

I drove back to Altair Street, Bay City. I put the gun back on Lavery's bathroom floor and called the police. They came fast, hard men with hard, cold eyes. I knew one of them – Detective Degarmo, the big man with a square face and very blue eyes. His boss was an angry little man called Webber. I sat in one of Lavery's chairs and answered their questions. I told them all about Kingsley, his wife, Bill Chess and Muriel, the black-and-white dress. All the time Degarmo watched me with cold eyes.

Then the police doctor arrived. Webber turned to Degarmo. 'OK, Al, you stay here with Marlowe. I'm going to look at the body with the doctor.'

He went out. I looked at Degarmo.

'How's Dr Almore this morning?' I said. 'What's he afraid of today?'

'You said you didn't know Almore.' Degarmo's eyes were angry.

'I didn't yesterday. But today I know a lot of things. Chris Lavery knew Mrs Almore, and he found her dead body. Perhaps he knew it wasn't suicide. Perhaps he knew that Dr Almore was the murderer, and that there was a police cover-up.'

Degarmo stood up and walked over to me. 'Say that again,' he said angrily.

I said it again.

He hit me very hard across the face with his open hand. He didn't break my nose, but that was because I have a very strong nose. I looked at him and said nothing.

He spoke through his teeth at me. 'I don't like private detectives. Get out of here, fast! And don't make trouble!'

Chapter 5   A Little Dance

When I got back to my flat, it was early evening. I washed my face and had a drink. Webber thought that Crystal Kingsley killed Lavery. I thought that was too easy. I phoned Redhead. 'Where do Florence Almore's parents live?' I asked her. She told me, and I went out to my car again.

Mr and Mrs Grayson were old and grey. They had tired grey faces and grey smiles. Very sad people. They listened to me quietly.

Mr and Mrs Grayson were old and grey. They had tired grey faces and grey smiles. Very sad people. They listened to me quietly.

'I'm interested in Dr Almore because his house is across the road from Chris Lavery's,' I said. 'You see, somebody shot Lavery this morning in his bathroom. Perhaps it was Dr Almore. You think he murdered your daughter a year and a half ago, right?'

'Yes,' said Mr Grayson. 'We know he killed her.'

'Why do you think that? And how do you know?' I asked quietly.

'Florence wasn't a very good wife, or daughter,' Mr Grayson said sadly. 'But she found Almore and his office nurse in bed together, and she wanted to make trouble for Almore. He didn't like that. Difficult for his job. So one night he killed her with drugs. He always had a lot of dangerous drugs in the house. It was easy for him. There was a police cover-up about it, we know that, too.'

'I heard that Almore's nurse put Mrs Almore to bed that night,' I said. 'Was that the same nurse?'

'Yes, it was,' said Mrs Grayson. 'We never saw the girl. But she had a pretty name. What was it, now? Just give me a minute.'

We gave her a minute. 'Mildred something,' she said.

I didn't move. 'Mildred Haviland, perhaps?' I said quietly.

Mrs Grayson smiled. 'Yes, that's right. Mildred Haviland.'

♦

At Bay City police station I asked at the desk for Webber. He didn't want to see me, but I said it was important. He took me into his office and we sat down.

'I want to talk about the Florence Almore suicide,' I said.

'Why?' asked Webber. 'That happened a year and a half ago. I'm working on the Lavery murder now. That happened today.'

'But I think Lavery is the key to the story,' I said. 'Listen, *One*: Muriel Chess's dead body came up in Little Fawn Lake yesterday. *Two*: I think Muriel Chess was Mildred Haviland. *Three*: Mildred Haviland was Dr Almore's office nurse a year and a half ago. *Four*: Mildred Haviland put Mrs Almore to bed on the night when she died. Was it suicide or murder? But Mildred Haviland left town soon after. Why was that? *Five*: Mildred Haviland then married and lived with Bill Chess at Little Fawn Lake *Six*: Bill Chess worked for Mr Kingsley up at the lake. *Seven*: Kingsley's wife sometimes slept in the same bed as Chris Lavery. *Eight*: Chris Lavery found Mrs Almore's dead body a year and a half ago.'

'I don't understand,' said Webber slowly.

'I don't understand *all* the story,' I said. 'I don't understand why,

21

'I don't understand all the story,' I said. 'I don't understand why, or how. But it's the same story.'

or how. But it's the same story. The same names go round and round in a little dance.' I lit a cigarette and looked at Webber. 'And Detective Degarmo doesn't like any questions about the Almores. He gets very angry. Why? Was there something . . . wrong about Mrs Almore's suicide?'

'OK,' said Webber. 'I wasn't in this office at the time of the Almore suicide. But there *was* something . . . not right. Perhaps somebody *did* murder Mrs Almore.'

'And Degarmo worked on the Almore suicide.'

'That's right.'

'And his name is Al. And the writing on Mildred Haviland's watch says, "Al to Mildred. With all my love." And a big man with a square face was up at Puma Point six weeks ago with a photo of Mildred Haviland.'

'OK, Marlowe,' Webber said tiredly. 'What do you want?'

'I want to show that Mrs Kingsley did *not* murder Lavery. I think Lavery died because he knew something about Dr Almore or Mildred Haviland. And when I show that Mrs Kingsley is not a murderer, I get five hundred dollars from Mr Kingsley.'

Webber smiled. 'OK,' he said.

'And Degarmo?'

Webber's face was sad. 'She was his wife at one time. Six or seven years ago. She gave him a very hard time.'

I sat very, very quietly and looked at him. 'Mildred Haviland was Degarmo's *wife*?'

'Yes. She's dangerous, that lady. She eats men for breakfast, but they love it. One smile from her, and men jump out of windows for her. Degarmo loved her then, and he loves her now.'

♦

I got back to my flat at about midnight. When I opened the door, I heard the phone. I walked across the room and answered it. It was Derace Kingsley.

'I heard from Crystal this evening. I'm coming round to your flat now. Be ready to move.' The phone went dead.

Chapter 6   Room 618

Kingsley arrived five minutes later. He didn't want to sit down and he didn't want a drink. He pulled out a brown envelope and gave it to me.

'Take this to Crystal,' he said. 'She's waiting for you now, in the Black Cat bar down in Bay City. There's five hundred dollars in that envelope. She's in trouble. She knows the police are looking for her. She must get out of town tonight, but she wants money.'

I put the envelope on the table. 'Not so fast,' I said. 'How does she know the police are looking for her? And did she kill Lavery? I'm not going to help a murderer.'

Kingsley's eyes were very unhappy. 'I know that's difficult for you,' he said quietly. 'But what can I do? Perhaps she killed Lavery, perhaps she didn't. I didn't speak to her on the phone. The girl in my office took the call. Crystal didn't want to talk to me, and I didn't want to talk to her. I don't want to see her again. But she *is* my wife.'

I walked across to the window and thought for a minute. 'OK,' I said. 'I'm going. I want to hear her story. But I give murderers to the police, OK? Now, how is she going to know me?'

Kingsley smiled for the first time. 'Thanks, Marlowe,' he said. 'Crystal says her hair's light brown now, and short – not long and yellow. And you can wear my scarf. She knows that.' He took it off and gave it to me. It was green and yellow and red. The colours hit me in the eye.

♦

24

Kingsley didn't want to sit down and he didn't want a drink. He pulled out a brown envelope and gave it to me.

At one-fifteen in the morning the Black Cat bar was quiet – only five or six people were at the tables. By the door was a small woman with light-brown hair. She wore a yellow dress and a short grey coat. She saw my scarf first, and then me. We walked out into the street together and stopped by a shop window.

'Give me the money,' she said.

'I want to hear your story.'

'No.'

'No story, no money.'

She turned her head away and said nothing for a minute. Then, 'OK. Come to the Granada Hotel. Room 618. It's in the next street. Come in ten minutes.' She walked away down the street. I stood by the window and followed her with my eyes.

Room 618 was a big sitting-room. There was a half-open door at the back, perhaps to the bedroom and bathroom. I sat down and looked at Mrs Kingsley very carefully. I had one, not very good photo of her, but I had a good picture in my head. Crystal Kingsley was young and pretty and not very clever. The woman in front of me was young and pretty – and very, very clever. She gave me a quick, little-girl smile, and I watched her quiet eyes carefully.

'Give me the money, please,' she said.

'The story first,' I said. 'You left your car in San Bernardino and you met Lavery there. You sent Kingsley a letter from El Paso. What did you do then?'

'Why do you want to know?'

'Do you want the money?'

She looked at me for a minute, then she told me her story. She left Lavery in El Paso, and he went home to Bay City. She didn't want to stay with him. After that, she moved about. She stayed in hotels, here and there. She wanted to be quiet, to think, she said.

I listened. It was a good story and she told it well. Clever Mrs Kingsley.

26

We walked out into the street together and stopped by a shop window. 'Give me the money,' she said.

'Before you left Little Fawn Lake,' I said, 'did you have a fight with Muriel Chess? About Bill.'

'Bill Chess? What are you talking about?'

'Bill says you went to bed with him.'

'Don't be stupid! That dirty little man!'

'Perhaps he is. The police think he's a murderer, too. Of his wife. We found Muriel's dead body in the lake. After a month.'

She put a finger between her teeth and watched me carefully. 'What a sad story,' she said slowly.

'But Muriel Chess was Mildred Haviland. And Mildred Haviland was Dr Almore's office nurse. And Lavery lives across the road from Dr Almore. So you understand that I wanted to talk to you.'

'I can't help you about Muriel.'

'No,' I said. 'Oh well, here's the money from Kingsley.' I gave her the envelope and sat down again. I watched her eyes and said quietly, 'That was a very pretty blue hat. Your hair was a darker brown this morning, but those nice legs are the same. I always remember a woman's legs. I don't think you saw me in my car outside Lavery's house this morning.'

She went very quiet. 'So you think I shot Chris Lavery?' she said slowly.

'I don't think it. I know it.'

'What are you going to do now?'

'Give you to the police.'

Suddenly, there was a gun in her hand, and she laughed. Not a nice laugh.

'Stand up,' she said.

I stood up, and gave her a weak smile. 'Detective meets murderer, and murderer shoots detective. Is that it?' I asked. 'But you're not very good with guns. You're standing too near me.'

She didn't like that, and her eyes moved angrily. I hit her gun hand hard and kicked her feet at the same time. The gun hit the floor, and I caught her arms behind her back. She was strong, and

Suddenly, there was a gun in her hand, and she laughed. Not a nice laugh.

fought and kicked. Suddenly I heard a new sound, but I had no time to look. I knew that there was a man behind me and that he was a big man. Then something hit me on the back of the head and everything went black.

Chapter 7   Little Fawn Lake

When I opened my eyes, I was on my back on the floor. I sat up slowly, and my head went round and round. I closed my eyes again and waited. After two or three minutes I opened them, and began to stand up. It took me a long time. Suddenly I was an old man of ninety-five.

And where was I? I remembered a girl, a girl with light-brown hair and quiet eyes. I looked round the room. She was on the floor by the door to the bedroom. Her eyes were open, but she didn't see me. She didn't see anything, and she didn't say anything. There was a long kitchen knife in her throat, and the light-brown hair and the yellow dress were all red.

Murder-a-day Marlowe, I thought. This was my third dead body, and I wasn't happy about it. You can find one murdered body, or perhaps two, and walk away. But when you find three bodies in two days, the police start to get very interested in you.

The hotel was very quiet, but suddenly I heard sounds of cars in the street. I went to the window and looked out carefully. Police cars. A lot of them. They stopped outside the hotel.

Quickly I found my coat, Kingsley's scarf and the envelope of money. I left the room fast and went down at the back of the building. I found the door to the garage under the hotel, opened it quietly and went through. I began to run to my car – but a big hand came out of the dark and caught my arm. And somebody said quietly into my ear, 'Let's take a walk, Marlowe.'

I looked round, into the very blue eyes of Detective Degarmo.

This was my third dead body and I wasn't happy about it.

◆

We drove away from the hotel and then stopped and talked in my car. Degarmo was in trouble with his boss, Webber, and he didn't want Webber to find me.

'What happened, Marlowe? There's a dead woman up in Room 618. Somebody called the police ten minutes ago.'

I lit a cigarette and told him my story – about the call to Kingsley, my meeting with Mrs Kingsley, the man in the room, the hit on my head.

He looked at me carefully. 'Did you see this man?'

'No. He was a big man, but I didn't see his face. This yellow-and-green scarf was on the floor.' I showed it to Degarmo. 'I saw it on Kingsley earlier this evening. Perhaps Kingsley killed her. She made a lot of trouble for him.' I watched his face.

He thought about it for a minute. 'OK, I'm interested,' he said.

He looked at me. 'I want to find this murderer before Webber finds him. And then perhaps I can get out of trouble. Let's go and talk to Kingsley, eh? Where does he live?'

But Kingsley was not at home. We found a phone and I called Redhead, but she didn't know. Then I phoned Policeman Jim Patton up at Puma Point. It was now half past four in the morning. Half an hour later Jim Patton called me back. Yes, he said, there was a light on in Kingsley's house at Little Fawn Lake and his car was outside.

We drove up into the mountains, stopped, ate some breakfast and drove again. After a long time Degarmo spoke: 'That dead girl in the lake up there. That was my girl. Mildred. Webber told me last night. I'd like to get my hands on that Bill Chess.'

'Don't make more trouble,' I said. 'You covered up for Mildred a year and a half ago. When she murdered Dr Almore's wife.'

He turned his head and looked at me. He laughed, but his eyes were hard and angry.

'A dangerous lady,' I said, 'but you loved her. She put Florence Almore to bed, and gave her a killer drug. When Almore came home, his wife was dead. But you and he covered up for Mildred – Almore, because he was afraid, and you, because you loved her. Am I right?'

The big man didn't say a word.

'Then you sent Mildred away. So she went away, and married Bill Chess. But Little Fawn Lake isn't a very exciting place, and after about a year Mildred wanted to leave. She didn't have any money, so she wrote to Almore. No address, just send money to Mildred at Puma Point. But that's a dangerous game. The first time it's fifty dollars. The next time it's five hundred dollars. Almore didn't like that, so he sent you up to Puma Point with a photograph. I think Mildred was a little afraid of you, Degarmo. But you didn't find her. Right?'

Degarmo looked out of the window. After a minute or two he said, 'OK. Let's forget it. It's all finished now.'

We found a phone and I phoned Jim Patton up at Puma Point. It was now half past four in the morning.

We drove on to Little Fawn Lake. The sun was up now, and the mountains were very beautiful in the early-morning light.

Chapter 8   Every Man Jumped

Jim Patton met us on the road near Kingsley's house. He had a young policeman with him, a boy called Andy. We got out of the car.

'Hi, Jim,' I said.

Jim Patton gave me his big friendly smile. 'How are you, son?' he said. He looked at Degarmo.

'This is Detective Degarmo of the Bay City Police,' I said.

'Somebody murdered Kingsley's wife in Bay City last night,' said Degarmo. 'I want to talk to him about it.'

'You think Mr Kingsley killed her?' Jim Patton asked.

We told him the story, and then the three of us moved up to Kingsley's house. Degarmo had a gun under his jacket. Patton had a gun, too, but I don't like carrying guns. They can get you into trouble.

We pushed open the door and went in. Kingsley was in a chair, his eyes closed and a whisky bottle on the table next to him. His face was tired and grey.

Degarmo spoke first. 'Your wife's dead, Kingsley. And you left your scarf behind in Room 618. That was stupid.' He turned to me. 'Show him the scarf,' he said.

I got out the yellow, green and red scarf, and put it on a table. Kingsley looked at it, then at me, then at Degarmo.

'I don't understand,' he said. 'That's my scarf, but Marlowe wore it when he went down to Bay City. My wife didn't know him, and – '

Degarmo made an angry sound and turned to me. 'You didn't tell me that,' he said quickly.

'You didn't want to know,' I said. 'You wanted Kingsley to be the

34

Jim Patton met us on the road near Kingsley's house. He had a young policeman with him called Andy. We got out of the car.

murderer. That was a nice, easy answer.' I looked at Kingsley. 'I only saw your wife in a photograph. But I *did* see her before last night. She was the woman in the blue hat outside Lavery's house yesterday morning. I told you. Remember?'

'I didn't hear about a woman in a blue hat,' said Degarmo angrily. 'So Mrs Kingsley *did* murder Lavery, then.'

'No,' I said. 'She didn't murder Lavery. And you know that better than anybody. She didn't shoot Lavery yesterday morning, because she died a month ago. Crystal Kingsley was the dead woman in Little Fawn Lake. And the woman in the Granada Hotel last night was Mildred Haviland, and Mildred Haviland was Muriel Chess. So Mildred Haviland murdered Chris Lavery yesterday morning, and somebody murdered Mildred last night.'

For a long time nobody spoke. Then Jim Patton said slowly, 'But Bill Chess thought the woman in the lake was his wife.'

'After a month in the water?' I said. 'The body wore his wife's clothes and had the same long yellow hair. Everybody thought it was Muriel. Why not?'

'Finish the story, son,' Jim Patton said. He watched Degarmo all the time. He didn't look at Kingsley.

So I told them. They all listened to me very carefully. Degarmo's face was white and his eyes were hard and cold. I told them about Florence Almore's murder a year and a half ago, and about the police cover-up. 'Mildred was a very dangerous lady,' I said. 'After the first murder, the next murder is easy. She wanted to leave Little Fawn Lake, and she wanted money. Almore didn't give her any money. But Crystal Kingsley was rich, and Mildred found her in bed with her man, Bill. Mildred didn't like that. So she murdered Mrs Kingsley and put her body in the lake. Then she pretended to be Mrs Kingsley. She took her money, her clothes and her car, and went down to San Bernardino. There she met trouble – Chris Lavery. Lavery knew that she was Muriel Chess, and not Crystal Kingsley. But Mildred was a clever girl. When she said "jump",

The room was very quiet.

every man jumped for her. So she took Lavery away with her, and wrote to Kingsley from El Paso.'

I stopped. Nobody said anything. Nobody moved. Kingsley looked at the floor, Patton looked at Degarmo, and Degarmo looked at nothing. I lit a cigarette. 'But then Lavery went home to Bay City. She stayed near him, because he was dangerous to her. He *knew* that she wasn't Crystal Kingsley. Then I began to ask questions about Mrs Kingsley, and that was the finish for Lavery. Mildred went down to his house and shot him in the bathroom.'

I stopped again, and Patton said slowly, 'So who killed Mildred, son? Do we know that, too?'

The room was very quiet. 'Let's say that it was a very unhappy man. He loved Mildred, he helped her many times, but it wasn't easy for him. He wanted to stop the murders – three were too many. But he didn't want everybody to know her story. Let's say it was Degarmo.'

Degarmo moved away from the window, and his gun was in his hand. 'That's a very interesting story, Marlowe.' He smiled, but not with his eyes. 'How did I find her, then?'

'I think Almore saw her outside Lavery's house one day. He told you, then you followed her to the Granada Hotel. Easy for a detective.'

'Yeah,' Degarmo said. He began to move to the door. 'Well, I'm leaving now. And no fat old policeman is going stop me.'

'Don't do it, son,' Jim Patton said to him quietly.

Degarmo laughed, and looked at the gun in his right hand. Patton didn't move. But his gun spoke for him, and Degarmo's gun flew out of his hand and hit the floor. Degarmo turned, and ran to the door.

We went to the window and watched. 'I can't shoot a man in the back,' Patton said sadly. 'He's going to take Andy's car. But he can't get out of these mountains. We can stop all the roads.'

Degarmo ran to Andy's car, got in and drove away fast. I turned and looked at Kingsley. He stood up, got a new bottle of whisky

A hundred feet down the mountain was Andy's little red car. The men down there carefully pulled something big and heavy out of the car.

from the cupboard, went into the bedroom and closed the door. Patton and I went quietly out of the house.

♦

We drove down to Puma Point. On the road outside the village there were some cars and a lot of people. We stopped and got out. A man came over to us.

'There's a car down there, Jim,' he said. 'The man drove too fast and went off the road down the mountain. They're pulling him out now.'

We went and looked. A hundred feet down the mountain was Andy's little red car. The men down there carefully pulled something big and heavy out of the car.

It was the dead body of a man.

ACTIVITIES

Chapters 1–2

Before you read

1 Look at the Word List at the back of this book. Answer these questions with words from the list.

    a When there is a murder or a suicide, what do the police find?

    b Do you put a scarf round your throat or your feet?

    c Which word means 'woman'?

    d Which is better: to be lucky or to be in trouble?

2 Read the Introduction to the book and answer these questions.

    a Who is Philip Marlowe looking for?

    b Where does this story happen?

    c Why does Marlowe have to find answers quickly?

While you read

4 Write the names of the people from the story. Who:

    a is Derace Kingsley's wife? ....

    b is Kingsley's wife's lover? ....

    c works for Mr Kingsley and went to bed
with Kingley's wife? ....

    d lives across the street from Lavery? ....

    e is Bill Chess's wife? ....

    f is a policeman in Puma Point, near Little
Fawn Lake? ....

After you read

5 Talk to another student. What do you know about Crystal Kingsley, Chris Lavery, Dr Almore and Bill Chess?

6 Why are these important in the story?

    a June 12th

    b Crystal's letter to her husband

    c Crystal and Muriel's hair, eyes and body

Chapters 3–4

Before you read

7   Look at the pictures in Chapters 3 and 4 and answer these
    questions.
    a Who gives Mildred a watch?
    b Who does Marlowe watch from inside his car?
    c What does Marlowe see when he opens the door?

While you read

8   What happens first? What happens next? Write 1–8.

    a Marlowe finds a watch in Bill Chess's house from
        Al to Mildred and takes it to Jim Patton's office in
        Puma Point.   .....
    b Marlowe finds Lavery's dead body and a small,
        lady's gun on the floor next to him.   .....
    c At the Prescott Hotel, Marlowe learns more about
        Crystal and Lavery on the night of June 12th.   .....
    d A Los Angeles policeman goes to the hotel in Puma
        Point and asks questions about Mildred Haviland.   .....
    e Marlowe watches a woman when she leaves
        Lavery's house.   .....
    f Marlowe learns more about the night Florence Almore
        died in her car in the garage and about Lavery.   .....
    g Marlowe finds an expensive black-and-white dress
        in Lavery's cupboard.   .....

After you read

9   What do you know about:
    a Mildred Haviland and Muriel Chess?
    b Crystal Kingsley's clothes on June 12th and the woman's
        clothes in Lavery's cupboard?
    c Dr Almore's work with women on drugs and his wife?
10 What happens to Mrs Almore? Why? Who is Al?

Chapter 5

Before you read

11 Al Degarrno and his boss, Webber, ask Marlowe questions. Why don't they like Marlowe? What will happen next?

12 Which of these does Marlowe want to learn more about? Why?

    a How did Mrs Almore die?

    b What drugs did Mrs Almore take?

    c Who murdered Lavery?

    d What was Detective Degarmo's wife's name?

    e Who were Crystal Kingsley's other lovers?

While you read

13 Put these words in the sentences.

    cover-up   husband   murder   nurse   suicide

    a Mrs Almore's parents, Mr and Mrs Grayson, know about a police ....

    b Mildred Haviland was Dr Almore's .... and she put Mrs Almore in bed on her last night.

    c Webber didn't want to talk to Marlowe about Florence Almore's ....

    d 'Perhaps somebody *did* .... Mrs Almore,' Webber tells Marlowe.

    e Degarmo was Mildred Haviland's .... and he loves her to this day.

After you read

14 Who says these things? Why?

    a 'Florence wasn't a very good wife, or daughter.'

    b 'The same names go round and round in a little dance.'

    c 'She's dangerous, that lady. She eats men for breakfast, but they love it.'

15 Work with another student. Have this conversation.

    Student A: You are Marlowe. You go to Webber's office because you want to learn about Mrs Almore's suicide and Lavery.

    Student B: You are Webber. Tell Marlowe about Mildred Haviland and her suicide.

16 Discuss: Who do you think is the lady in the lake? Why? And how did she get there?

Chapters 6–7

Before you read

17 Look at the pictures in Chapters 6 and 7 and answer these questions.
   a What is Mr Kingsley wearing round his throat?
   b What is he giving to Marlowe?
   c What is Marlowe wearing round his throat when he meets the woman in the street?

18 Marlowe has a photo of Crystal with Lavery but it is not a good photo. Will he know her when he sees her? Why (not)?

While you read

19 Are these sentences right (✓) or wrong (✗)?
   a Crystal phones her husband's office and speaks to him.   .....
   b Crystal's hair is short now and the colour is light brown.   .....
   c At one-fifteen in the morning, Marlowe meets Crystal at the Granada Hotel in Room 618.   .....
   d Marlowe remembers Crystal's legs from earlier in the day but her hair is lighter now.   .....
   e Crystal gets a gun but Marlowe hits it out of her hand.   .....
   f A man hits Marlowe on the head, so Marlowe doesn't see Crystal's murderer.   .....
   g Marlowe leaves the hotel room with Kingsley's scarf, the envelope of money and the gun.   .....
   h Marlowe tells Degarmo about Kingsley's scarf in the hotel room and about Kingsley's trouble with his wife.   .....
   i After Degarmo tells Marlowe about his girl Mildred in the lake, Marlowe talks about the cover-up.   .....
   j After Mildred kills Almore's wife with drugs, Degarmo sends Mildred away.   .....

20 Talk with another student about the man in Crystal's hotel room. Who was he, do you think? Why does he kill Crystal?

21 At half-past four in the morning, Marlowe phones policeman Jim Patton at Puma Point. Why?

Chapter 8

Before you read

22 What will we learn about the Lady in the Lake, do you think?

23 Look at the pictures in Chapter 8. Will there be trouble for Degarmo, do you think? What and why (not)?

While you read

24 Which of these are about Mildred? Put a (✓) next to the right answers.

a She died a month ago.	.....
b She is the lady in the lake.	.....
c She is the woman in the Granada Hotel.	.....
d She is Muriel Chess.	.....
e She murders Chris Lavery.	.....
f She murders Florence Almore.	.....
g She murders Mrs Kingsley and puts her body in the lake.	.....
h She pretends to be Mrs Kingsley and meets Lavery in San Bernardino.	.....
i She writes the letter to Mr Kingsley from El Paso.	.....

After you read

25 Discuss these questions.

   a What happens to Detective Degarmo?

   b Is he a bad man?

   c What does he know from the start of the story?

   d Why doesn't Patton shoot him when he runs away?

   e Why does Mildred Haviland pretend to be Crystal Kingsley?

   f How does she do this?

   g Why does nobody understand this for a long time?

   h How does Marlowe find out?

Writing

26 Write the names of the people Marlowe meets in Chapters 1 and 2 and write two or three sentences about each person.

27 Mr Kingsley gives Marlowe a letter for Bill Chess. Marlowe shows it to Chess in Chapter 2. Write Mr Kingsley's letter.

28 Was Muriel's letter to her husband, Bill, a goodbye letter or a suicide letter? What did she write? Write her last letter.

29 Write a story for the Puma Point newspaper about Bill Chess's wife. How did Chess find her? Who do the police want to question?

30 What does Marlowe learn about Dr Almore and his wife, Florence? Write a letter from Marlowe to Florence's parents and tell them about Florence's last night.

31 Marlowe tells Degarmo about the call to Kingsley, his meeting with Mrs Kinglsey, the man in the room and the hit on his head. Write Marlowe's story.

32 Write a newspaper story about Detective Degarmo. Write about his life and about his car accident.

33 Write about a person in the story. Do you like him/her? Why (not)?

WORD LIST *with example sentences*

ago (adv) My brother is 19. He left school two years *ago*.

body (n) She jumped off the bridge, and the police found her *body* in the river two days later.

cover-up (n) The police killed him. But there was a *cover-up* so nobody knew about it.

drug (n) She drinks a lot and she smokes and takes *drugs*.

just (adv) Can I have some money? I don't want a lot – *just* $10.

lady (n) This *lady* is my wife.

lake (n) We walked round the *lake* and then we swam in it.

luck (n) Good *luck* in the game. I hope you'll be *lucky* and win.

murder (n/v) He's dead, and it wasn't an accident. It was *murder*.

must (v) We haven't got any food in the house. We *must* buy some.

nurse (n) Twenty doctors and a hundred *nurses* work in the hospital.

pretend (v) She *pretended* to love him, but she only wanted his money.

private (adj) He's not a policeman; he's a *private* detective. He works for me.

scarf (n) It was cold, so he put on a thick coat, a hat and a long red *scarf*.

shoot (v) He's got a gun! He's going to *shoot* us!

suicide (n) Did somebody push her, or did she jump? I mean, was it murder or *suicide*?

throat (n) Somebody cut his *throat* from ear to ear.

together (adv) Those two are good friends; they always sit *together*.

trouble (n) You're in *trouble*. The police are looking for you.

whisky (n) *Whisky* is a strong drink from Scotland.

The Birds
Daphne du Maurier

Nat and his family live near the sea. Nat watches the birds over the sea. Suddenly the weather is colder, and there is something strange about the birds. They are angry. They start to attack. They want to get into the house. They want to kill.

The Room in the Tower and Other Stories
Rudyard Kipling and Others

Three stories, three ghosts. A young woman marries an older man. His first wife is dead. Or is she . . . ? Why does a dead man walk through his house each night? An old woman has a house with a tower. Why does she visit a young man in his dreams?

Simply Suspense

There are three exciting short stories in this book. They are all about . . . fear! Three people are in dangerous places. What can they do? Will anybody help them?

There are hundreds of Penguin Readers to choose from – world classics, film adaptations, modern-day crime and adventure, short stories, biographies, American classics, non-fiction, plays ...

For a complete list of all Penguin Readers titles, please contact your local Pearson Longman office or visit our website.

www.penguinreaders.com

Longman Dictionaries

Express yourself with confidence!

*Longman has led the way in ELT dictionaries since 1935.
We constantly talk to students and teachers around the
world to find out what they need from a learner's dictionary.*

Why choose a Longman dictionary?

Easy to understand

Longman invented the Defining Vocabulary – 2000 of the most
common words which are used to write the definitions in our
dictionaries. So Longman definitions are always clear and easy
to understand.

Real, natural English

All Longman dictionaries contain natural examples taken from
real-life that help explain the meaning of a word and show you
how to use it in context.

Avoid common mistakes

Longman dictionaries are written specially for learners, and we
make sure that you get all the help you need to avoid common
mistakes. We analyse typical learners' mistakes and include
notes on how to avoid them.

Innovative CD-ROMs

Longman are leaders in dictionary CD-ROM innovation. Did
you know that a dictionary CD-ROM includes features to help
improve your pronunciation, help you practice for exams and
improve your writing skills?

**For details of all Longman dictionaries, and to choose
the one that's right for you, visit our website:**

www.longman.com/dictionaries